The Whodunit
Detective Agency

The Movie Theater Mystery

GROSSET & DUNLAP
Penguin Young Readers Group
An Imprint of Penguin Random House LLC

Original title: Biografmysteriet
Text by Martin Widmark
Original cover and illustrations by Helena Willis

English language edition copyright © 2016 Penguin Random House LLC. Original edition published by Bonnier Carlsen Bokförlag, Sweden, 2004. Text copyright © 2004 by Martin Widmark. Illustrations copyright © 2004 by Helena Willis. Published in 2016 by Grosset & Dunlap, an imprint of Penguin Random House LLC, 345 Hudson Street, New York, New York 10014. GROSSET & DUNLAP is a trademark of Penguin Random House LLC. Manufactured in China.

Library of Congress Cataloging-in-Publication Data is available.

ISBN 978-0-448-48078-7 (pb)   10 9 8 7 6 5 4 3 2 1
ISBN 978-0-448-48079-4 (hc)   10 9 8 7 6 5 4 3 2 1

The Whodunit? Detective Agency

The Movie Theater Mystery

Martin Widmark
illustrated by Helena Willis

Grosset & Dunlap
An Imprint of Penguin Random House

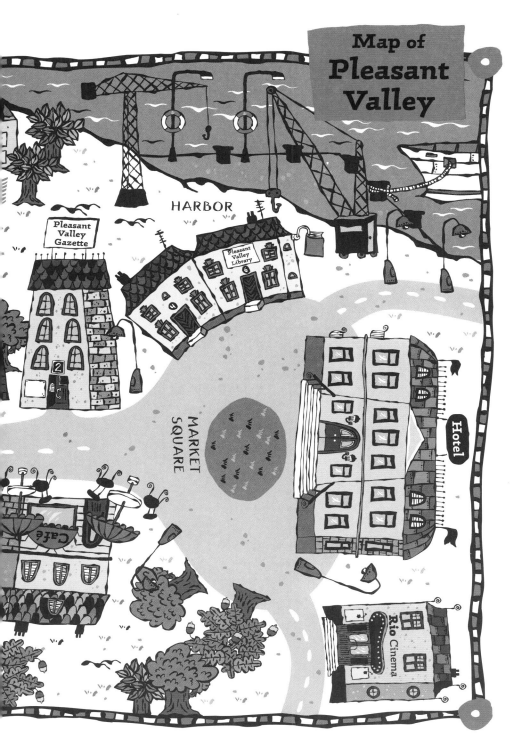

The Movie Theater Mystery

The books in *The Whodunit Detective Agency* series are set in the charming little town of Pleasant Valley. It's the sort of close-knit community where nearly everyone knows one another. The town and the characters are all fictional, of course . . . or are they?

The main characters, Jerry and Maya, are classmates and close friends who run a small detective agency together.

The people:

Jerry

Maya

Miss Bloom

Derek

Zorba

Popcorn Pete

CHAPTER 1

A Singing Dog

"Look!" said Maya. "It's happened again!" She passed Jerry the newspaper and jabbed at an article. The two friends were relaxing in their favorite comfy armchairs in Maya's basement. Maya's basement: otherwise known as the Whodunit Detective Agency Headquarters. They kept everything they needed to run their agency there.

Jerry read the newspaper while Maya grabbed their scrapbook and a pair of scissors.

The scrapbook was full of articles they had found about all sorts of crimes.

"Another dog stolen." Jerry sighed when he finished the article.

"That makes the third one this week. Look at this," said Maya, opening the scrapbook in front of Jerry.

She pointed to two other articles that she had pasted under her own headline: "Disappearing Dogs."

"There's *got* to be a connection between all these thefts," said Jerry.

Maya picked up the scrapbook and nodded. "Let's read the article again and see if there are any similarities between the cases."

They each took out their notebooks. As

they read, Jerry and Maya wrote down the
main points in each article. Then they
compared what they had written.

"Only small dogs have
disappeared," noted Jerry.
"No big dogs. I wonder
why?"

"Well, it's easier to run
off with a small dog," said

Maya. "And a small dog probably isn't as dangerous as a big dog."

"The dogs have been stolen all over town," said Jerry.

"That's right: outside the library, by the church, and in front of the hotel," continued Maya, as she checked over her notes.

"The dogs were all stolen at around the same time, between seven and seven thirty at night," said Jerry.

"The owners had left the dogs unattended for only a few minutes," Maya said.

"But still long enough for the dog thief to strike," said Jerry, scratching his nose thoughtfully with his pen.

Maya snipped out the most recent article from the paper and pasted it into the scrapbook.

"What else do we know?" asked Jerry.

"According to the paper, each dog owner received a mysterious phone call shortly after the disappearance," said Maya. "None of them recognized the voice on the other end of the line. The caller demanded that each owner pay one thousand dollars—or they will never see their pets again."

"The owners must be frantic!" said Jerry.

"And the dogs, too." Maya sighed. "Someone rotten enough to steal a dog is probably rotten enough to treat them poorly."

"Read it again, Maya, and let's see if we missed anything," said Jerry. He closed his eyes to

LOST DOGS AND NO LEADS

"I must get my Doodle Bug back," said a desperate Ivy Rose, who was shocked to discover that her dog had been stolen from outside of the Pleasant Valley Hotel on Wednesday.

The thief called Ms. Rose late yesterday evening, demanding $1,000 for the return of Doodle Bug. Fighting back tears, Ivy Rose told the Pleasant Valley Gazette's reporter that the little poodle was her only companion. They spent so much time together that she had even taught him to sing! When Ms. Rose whistles, Doodle Bug joins in with a tuneful howl. She is now begging the thief to give the dog back. "I'm lost without my Doodle Bug!" she said.

Ms. Rose's pup is the third in a rash of doggy disappearances in the last week. The police have no leads and advise dog owners to be aware.

concentrate. Maya straightened up, cleared
her throat, and began to read.

Maya shut the book with a snap. Jerry
jumped. One look at her face and he could
tell that she was angry. Very angry.

"We've got to do something," she said. "We've got to stand up for those innocent dogs!"

The two detectives slouched in their armchairs and thought about what they *could* do. But they didn't come up with any good ideas. Finally, Jerry said, "The dogs won't come back just because we're sitting here worrying. Let's take a break and clear our heads. That new cowboy movie opened at the Rio Cinema today. Maybe it will give us some ideas. Come on, Maya! Let's go!"

Maya sighed and got up from

The Whistling Cowboy

First Showing: 5 p.m.
Second Showing: 7 p.m.

her armchair. She put the scrapbook down on the desk.

"You're probably right," she said. "A change of scenery will do me good. I'm too angry to think straight now! What kind of person would be cruel enough to steal someone's pet?"

The newspaper articles made it clear: Pleasant Valley had a criminal on the loose. Maya had a feeling their detective agency would soon have a new case to solve!

CHAPTER 2

Chaos in the Line

Maya's bike had a flat tire so she and Jerry walked to the movie theater.

Summer was officially over and the leaves on the trees had begun to change color. But it was still warm and pleasant outside. As they neared the post office they saw the police chief.

He was enjoying the last warm rays of the day's sun. Jerry and Maya walked up and said hello.

"Well, hello," said the police chief. "Where are my favorite detectives going on such a lovely afternoon?"

"We're going to check out the new cowboy movie at the Rio," said Maya.

"Lucky you," said the police chief. "I'm

looking for the dreaded dog thief, myself. I don't suppose you've seen anything suspicious?"

The police chief was hoping Jerry and Maya could help him out, just as they had on a couple of other tricky cases he'd investigated.

"We don't know anything other than what's in the paper," replied Maya. "One thousand dollars ransom for each dog—that's a lot of money."

"The first two owners have already paid," revealed the police chief. "They put the money into an untraceable account. They did their part, but the thief did not: The dogs haven't been returned. And now the thief is demanding money for the third dog by tomorrow."

"How awful," said Jerry. "But," he said, looking at his watch, "we have to get a move on, Maya, if we're going to make the movie."

"Let me know if you find out anything," the police chief called after them.

Maya and Jerry continued down Church Street, past Mohammed Carat's jewelry shop and Pleasant Valley's lovely café.

When they reached Market Square they saw that there were tons of people in front of the movie theater.

They went into the Rio and bought two tickets from the lady at the box office. The doors to the theater were open, and the manager was tearing tickets in the doorway. Jerry and Maya were at the end of the line.

Next Week!
gman Festival!
Mon.-Sat.

There was a bottleneck by the door, and several people were getting restless. Somebody said, "Hey! You were behind me! No cuts!"

Jerry and Maya stood on tiptoe to get a better view. Right away they saw an angry and bad-tempered man trying to sneak his way into the movie. They recognized him immediately. It was Bert

Anderson, the receptionist from the town's hotel.

"Hold it right there," said the cinema manager, as he grabbed hold of Bert Anderson.

"You'll have to come back this evening. This show is sold out."

He took a firm hold of Bert Anderson's coat collar and pushed him toward the doors. But before Bert got completely thrown out, he made one last attempt at getting into the movie.

Suddenly, over the noise of the crowd, a ripping sound was heard. In his rush, Bert had pulled the pocket of the manager's jacket right off! Tons of money—coins and bills—fell to the floor.

The manager looked at the money on the floor and then at Bert Anderson. He was furious.

Bert realized that he was never going to get in now and crept out through the exit.

"There's as much action here as there was in the Wild West." Maya laughed.

After the manager gathered his money, he returned to his place and tore Jerry and

Maya's tickets. He was agitated. He pulled back his sleeve and looked at his watch.

Wow! thought Maya, as the manager revealed a big, expensive gold watch on his wrist.

Maya saw something else as well: There were two playing cards tucked under the watch strap! The manager saw Maya looking and hastily pulled his sleeve down again.

Then he called to the woman at the box office: "Miss Bloom! Could you give Derek a call and find out where he is? He's supposed to start the film in two minutes."

"Sure thing," Miss Bloom replied. "But Zorba, you know how Derek's been recently—taking a taxi to work and arriving at the last minute."

Miss Bloom picked up the phone and dialed. Maya shrugged at all the commotion and followed Jerry into the theater.

They went to their favorite spot and sank into the comfy red seats.

"If the detective agency doesn't work out, we could try for jobs here," whispered Maya. "It looks like you can earn plenty of money as part of the movie-theater staff."

"Taxi to work, pockets full of money, and expensive watches," replied Jerry with a smile.

Derek, the theater's projectionist, must have arrived just in the nick of time, because at 4:50 p.m. the previews began, right on schedule.

On the steps next to the rows of seats stood a young man dressed in a red jacket and tall hat. A tray of snacks hung from a

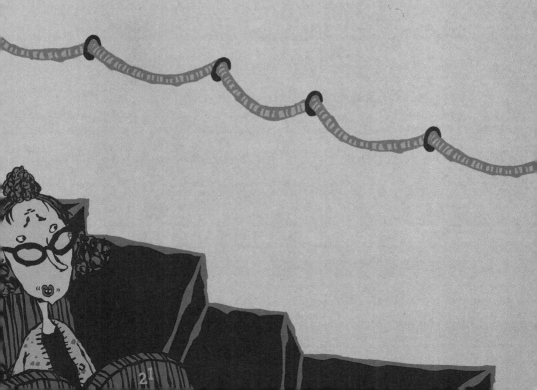

21

strap around his neck. Everyone at the theater knew him as Popcorn Pete.

"Oh, I'm starving," Maya said, and waved to the young man. She was in the mood for a snack. But no matter how much she waved, he didn't seem to see her.

Several other people in the audience did the same thing, but Popcorn Pete was watching the previews and didn't seem a bit interested in selling anything.

"If he can't be bothered to sell anything he's not going to keep that job for long," whispered Maya to Jerry, irritated. "But maybe he's as well-off as the rest of the staff and doesn't really *need* the job."

"*Sshh*," replied Jerry. The movie was starting.

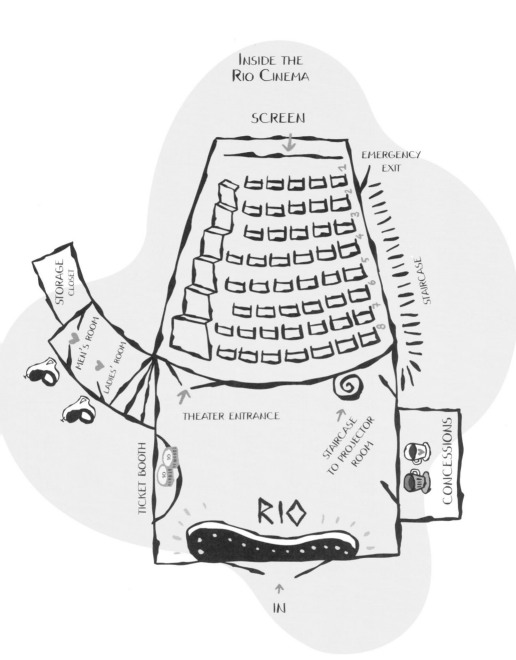

CHAPTER 3

Cards and Howls

When the movie started, Jerry and Maya watched Popcorn Pete take one of the seats reserved for the staff right at the front, near the emergency exit.

"That must be why he works here," whispered Jerry to Maya. "He gets to see the movies for free—and as many times as he wants."

Popcorn Pete slumped in his seat. Soon only his tall hat could be seen over the back of the seat.

The cowboy movie was excellent. It was about a gang of cowboys driving a herd of horses across the prairie. One of the cowboys could control horses just by whistling. If a horse looked as if it were going to run off,

the cowboy whistled and got it to stop.

Maya was impressed. She'd like to be able to whistle like that, too.

She turned to Jerry. But what was he doing? He wasn't even looking at the screen. He was leaning forward with his head to one side. He was listening to something down on the floor!

"What are you doing?" asked Maya.

"*Sshh*! I thought I heard something."

"Well of course you did. You're at the Rio watching a movie!"

"*Sssshh*!" said Jerry again and leaned even closer to the floor. "Wait here, Maya," he said and disappeared in the direction of the exit, crouching as he snuck down the aisle.

I wish I could whistle and stop him, thought Maya, watching Jerry as he slipped out the back doors.

When Jerry reached the empty hall outside the theater, he stood still and listened. Through a half-open door, he could hear Zorba and Miss Bloom talking. He stepped a little closer and listened at the door.

"I can't believe it," said Miss Bloom. "During every show for the past three years you and I have played cards, Zorba. And I haven't won *once* in all that time. I won't have any money left soon."

Jerry heard the sound of a stack of coins being pushed across a table and then the shuffling of cards.

"Oh, don't worry about it, Miss Bloom," said Zorba soothingly. "As they say, *Fortune comes and fortune goes, the lucky one knows no woes.*"

Jerry heard Miss Bloom sighing at Zorba's rhyme.

Sounds of the movie drifted from the theater: thundering hooves, neighing horses, and, of course, the cowboy whistling.

Now Jerry could clearly hear the sound he thought he heard in the theater! He followed the sound down the stairs, toward the bathrooms.

There were three doors downstairs: one to the women's bathroom, one to the men's, and a little further on, a third door, locked with a big, strong padlock.

Jerry walked up to the first door and listened.

If anyone walks up now I'll be thrown out of

the movie theater like Bert, he thought.
Here I am eavesdropping outside the women's bathroom!

But Jerry couldn't hear anything except some pipes gurgling. He moved on to the men's bathroom and looked in. He listened carefully but didn't hear anything strange.

There was only one door left: the one with the big padlock.

Jerry placed his ear to the keyhole. Now he could hear the sound again, loud and clear. A sad howling noise. It sounded just like a dog!

And not just any dog, thought Jerry. *It sounds like this one knows a special trick!*

He faced the keyhole and whistled softly, so that Zorba and Miss Bloom wouldn't hear him.

He waited a bit and after a moment the howling dog answered from behind the door!

"Ahem," he heard someone clear his throat behind him.

It was Zorba!

"Oh . . . ," said Jerry. He tried to think of something to say. "The bathroom . . ."

"The men's room is over there. Can't you read?" asked Zorba, sounding annoyed.

"My glasses," began Jerry. "I left my glasses in the theater . . ."

"Okay, okay, okay. But it's not that door in any case," said Zorba and pointed to the door with the padlock on. "That's a storeroom. Pretty useless these days: I don't even know where the key is. Now come on, hurry up. Otherwise you'll miss the whole movie."

Jerry disappeared into the men's room.

CHAPTER 4

The Screen Goes Dark

"**I** think I heard one of them," hissed Jerry to Maya, once he dropped back into his seat.

Maya looked at him in surprise. Jerry was turning out to be a strange movie date. Creeping around and talking during all the good parts. To think it was his idea to come to the movies in the first place!

"Heard one of what?" she asked impatiently. "Can't it wait until the movie's over?"

"Doodle Bug—the singing poodle from the newspaper!" whispered Jerry. "He's locked up downstairs! I could hear him whining from the storeroom."

Maya looked at Jerry, wide-eyed.

"What, really?" she asked, a little too

loudly. "Incredible! That must mean that . . ."

"*Shu-ush*!" hissed a man in the row behind them. "Keep it down!"

Jerry and Maya realized they would have to wait until the end of the movie to discuss the case.

They sat up straight in their seats and waited impatiently for the movie to end.

Maya wanted her snack more than ever, but it didn't look like she was going to get it before the movie was over.

Popcorn Pete was sitting perfectly still in his seat, probably completely absorbed by the movie. Just as Maya had been before she heard Jerry's news!

Suddenly, the screen went dark.

Maya tried to catch Jerry's eye, but she couldn't see anything.

The only light came from the emergency exit at the other side of the theater.

"What happened?"

"What was that?"

"Who turned out the lights?"

Everyone in the theater was wondering what had happened. Some sounded worried.

Then a voice rang out from the projection room behind them. It was Derek, the projectionist:

"Calm down, everyone! There's no emergency! The film reel snapped. Don't worry, I'll have it fixed in no time."

A few seconds later the film started rolling again. Thankfully there were no more problems.

When the movie ended the lights went up in the theater. The moviegoers got up from their seats and started walking toward the exit.

Popcorn Pete got up, too, and Maya frowned at him. Obviously he liked the movie more than selling snacks: His cheeks were red, but his tray was full.

Outside it had begun to get dark. Maya was nearly jumping with curiosity.

"Are you sure about what you heard?" she asked anxiously.

"Wait," said Jerry. "Not here. Someone might hear us. Let's go to the café and talk it over."

Jerry and Maya walked across the square

and sat at a table outside the café. They had a clear view of the Rio Cinema

The square was full of people out for a walk, enjoying the mild evening air. The light from the town's hotel illuminated the square and a ship's horn could be heard from the sea in the distance.

Sara Bernard, who worked in the café, walked over to Jerry and Maya and greeted them with a cheerful hello. Not so long ago, they had helped solve some burglaries at the café. Maya and Jerry each ordered a drink and a cinnamon bun.

"I'm almost positive. I'm sure I heard a dog behind that door!" said Jerry, leaning across the table. "But it could have belonged to one of the staff. Maybe one of them keeps their own dog in there."

"Do you remember Ivy Rose from the newspaper?" asked Jerry. "The one who lost her poodle? She said her dog would sing when she whistled to him. I whistled through the keyhole, and the dog inside immediately answered. I don't know if I'd call it singing, but I bet you my cinnamon bun that it's Doodle Bug locked up in the storeroom."

"But then that means . . . ," said Maya.

"Exactly: Someone from the Rio is the dog thief!"

"Let's go over what we know," said Maya. "And quickly. Who knows, maybe the other dogs are in there, too! A locked room is no place to keep an animal. Where do they keep the key to the storeroom?" asked Maya.

"The door was locked with a big padlock," Jerry told her, "but according to Zorba, the key has disappeared."

Jerry lowered his voice and gestured toward something with his head.

Maya turned and saw Bert Anderson walking by with determined strides.

Bert passed their table on his way to the movie theater.

"This time he wants to be first in line." Maya smiled.

CHAPTER 5

Cheats and Lazybones

"What do we know about the people who work at the Rio?" asked Jerry.

"Zorba the manager seems to have a surprising amount of money," said Maya. "He had a big gold watch on his arm and all kinds of money poured from his torn pocket."

"If he has *tons* of money that's because Miss Bloom from the box office is so *short* of money."

"What?" said Maya. She wasn't following Jerry's train of thought.

"Zorba and Miss Bloom

play cards while the movies are showing. They play for money! And I think that Zorba cheats with those extra cards he had tucked under his watch strap."

"That's terrible!" said Maya in amazement.

"Derek the projectionist has been coming to work in a taxi. Is he treating himself to a cab now that he's suddenly rich?" said Jerry thoughtfully.

"And Popcorn Pete doesn't seem a bit interested in selling snacks," said Maya. "Is he so well-off that he can afford the risk of losing his job? We can't be the only ones who have complained about him."

"So those three seem to have a lot of cash . . . but have any of them left the Rio during the time of the thefts?" asked Maya. She shook her head. "Around that time they're all busy in their different ways."

Sara came out with their order and put the drinks and buns on the table in front of them.

Jerry and Maya moved their chairs closer to each other, still keeping the Rio Cinema in their sights.

People had begun to gather for the 7:00 p.m. movie.

And in the crowd was the police chief. For a moment Maya and Jerry wondered if he too had traced the dog thief to the Rio Cinema. But then they saw him buy a ticket for the cowboy movie.

Maya took a big bite out of her cinnamon bun and thought for a moment. Finally she said, "The dogs have been stolen between seven and seven thirty in the evening. That falls during the second showing of the movie. The trail leads to the movie theater, but who can leave the Rio without being noticed?"

Jerry thought.

He couldn't understand how it was being done, either.

Zorba and Miss Bloom played cards with

each other. Popcorn Pete was sitting right at the front throughout the whole show. The projectionist, Derek, proved that he was right where he should be when he repaired the movie in just seconds.

Everyone was accounted for. Nobody seemed able to leave the theater without being noticed.

"If we have guessed right," said Maya finally, "someone who works at the Rio Cinema steals the dogs and then demands a ransom from their owners. Doodle Bug, and maybe even the other two dogs, are locked in the theater's storeroom. But none of the employees leaves the Rio Cinema during the movies, and that's when the dogs are stolen! How can that be?"

"There's only one way to find out the truth," said Jerry darkly.

"How?" asked Maya.

"By snooping," replied Jerry.

They waved to Sara Bernard for the bill. But Sara reminded them that all of their café meals were on the house as a thank you for catching the café thief.

Jerry and Maya got up from the table and strolled across the square toward the hotel.

They snuck around to the back of the hotel—a place where they had a good view of the Rio Cinema . . . but where no one could get a good view of them.

The perfect place for some detective work!

CHAPTER 6

The Ice Cream Consolation Prize

"What time is it?" asked Maya in a whisper. Jerry pressed a button on the side of his watch, and a little light came on.

"Seven on the dot," he replied.

"That's when the movie starts at the Rio," hissed Maya. "I'll bet that anyone who leaves the theater now is the dog thief!"

A young couple strolled past Maya and Jerry's hiding place. They were walking hand in hand, on their way to the boardwalk by the sea. To avoid being spotted, Jerry and Maya moved even farther back into the shadows, toward the cold stone walls of the hotel.

"Those two wouldn't have noticed us even if we had been dancing the tango in pajamas under that streetlight over there," said Maya.

"*Ssshh*!" whispered Jerry. "Look! Someone's coming out of the Rio!"

"It's probably Bert—thrown out again." Maya laughed quietly.

"Look, Maya! Over there!"

Maya looked so intently at the glass doors of the Rio that her eyes started to sting. And yes—one of the doors opened softly, and out came . . .

Zorba! The movie-theater manager. He stood for a moment in the doorway and listened to the sounds coming from the theater. Then he looked along the street and started walking toward the café.

Jerry and Maya crept along the side of the hotel, as silent as two shadows.

When Zorba walked past the tables outside the café, the two detectives scampered across the road and hid behind a tree.

The theater manager continued along Church Street, past Mohammed Carat's jewelry store.

Maya and Jerry trotted across the road to the church on the other side. Zorba continued to the post office.

Then he suddenly stopped and looked to the right and left.

Then he crossed the road! Straight toward Jerry and Maya!

They threw themselves down behind the wall of the church. Very slowly and carefully they peeked out around the corner. And there they saw him again.

The theater
manager had
stopped by the ice-
cream vendor—to buy
ice cream!

He was not in any
hurry. Taking his time,
he stood by the ice-
cream stand eating his ice
cream. Jerry and Maya
realized that Zorba could
not be the dog thief.

Someone who was planning to commit a crime would not stand and eat ice cream in full view of everyone on Church Street.

After Zorba had finished his cone he bought another and turned back toward the Rio. With ice cream in hand he walked right by Jerry and Maya's hiding place—so close, one of them could have taken a lick of his ice cream!

From where they were they could see him cross Market Square and go into the movie theater. The wind from the sea had picked up a little, and there was now hardly anybody left in the square.

"The ice cream must be for Miss Bloom," said Maya as they were walking along the street again.

"He must feel guilty about winning all that money from her," said Jerry.

Maya nodded slowly but didn't answer. She had noticed something.

"Look, Jerry," she said, pointing toward the other side of the hotel, down toward the harbor.

A hunched-over figure was scuttling along, clutching a large bundle.

Down by the lighted steps of the hotel, the person looked around anxiously, adjusted the bundle, and then hurried toward the doors of the cinema.

"Did you see who it was?" asked Maya excitedly.

"I think so . . . ," replied Jerry. "But minus a hat!"

Jerry and Maya saw the mysterious person disappear through the doors of the movie theater.

"Let's go," said Maya. "We need to get a move on!"

ZORBA'S WALK

1 LEAVES THE
RIO CINEMA

2 WALKS PAST THE
CAFÉ

3 WALKS PAST THE
JEWELER

4 WALKS PAST THE
POST OFFICE

5 CROSSES THE STREET

6 WALKS PAST THE
NEWSSTAND

7 WALKS BACK

8 CROSSING THE
MARKET SQUARE

CHAPTER 7

But—That's Impossible!

Maya and Jerry ran as fast as they could across Market Square. When they reached the Rio Cinema they stopped to catch their breaths. Now they needed to move without making a sound.

Maya opened one of the doors to the theater and let Jerry through. Then she crept in after him. They stopped in the foyer and listened. From inside the little room on the right, they could hear Miss Bloom and Zorba.

Jerry tiptoed forward and peered cautiously through an opening in the doorway. The manager and the woman from the box office had started playing cards again.

Zorba had his back to the door, and Miss Bloom was eating ice cream and concentrating on her cards. Jerry waved to tell Maya that the coast was clear. Quickly they hurried into the theater.

"One second," said Maya as she opened one of the doors to the auditorium. "I want to check something."

Jerry waited and shuffled his feet nervously. They had to hurry! What was she doing now? Jerry scowled after Maya. But when she returned and Jerry saw her look of surprise, his anger faded away.

"He's still in there," hissed Maya. "Hat and all!" She was stumped.

"But . . . ," said Jerry. "That's impossible. Derek is running the film, Miss Bloom and Zorba are playing cards. It must be him! Come on! We need to get a move on now!"

Jerry and Maya ran down the stairs to the bathrooms. When they got down there, they discovered that someone had unlocked the padlock to the storeroom. The padlock was hanging open on the door!

"Now's our chance!" said Jerry and rushed to the door.

"What are you doing?" asked Maya.

Jerry grabbed the padlock. Just then they heard someone moving toward the other side of the door.

"Hurry!" said Maya, who now realized Jerry's plan.

Jerry fumbled with the padlock—and dropped it on the floor!

"Quick—hold the door," he said to Maya.

Maya threw her shoulder against the door. And none too soon—someone was pulling on the door handle, trying to open it from the inside.

They heard angry muttering and then

rapid footsteps as the person inside took a run at the door!

Jerry picked up the padlock from the floor. Just as the unknown person inside threw themselves at the door with all their might, Jerry pushed on the padlock—it locked with a *click*!

The person on the other side hit the door with a great *thud*. But both the door and the padlock stood firm. The dog thief was trapped!

Maya and Jerry looked at each other with wide eyes. They were breathing heavily.

"Okay, now what?" asked Maya.

Jerry looked at her uneasily. He hadn't actually thought about that.

If the person inside went on throwing themselves at the door, either the door or the padlock would eventually give way.

"The police chief!" said Maya. "He's sitting in the theater. I'll run and grab him."

CHAPTER 8

As Good as a Lamppost

Maya opened the door to the theater and stepped into the dark. She searched the rows of seats to find the police chief. And there he was, in one of the back rows.

Maya waved to him but he was completely absorbed in the movie and didn't see her.

Maya had to reach past a few other people to tap the police chief on the shoulder.

"Oh, now you want to sell me candy?" he asked crossly.

"What's that?" asked Maya.

"Oh, I thought you were Popcorn Pete." The police chief laughed. "I've been trying to get his attention for ages!"

"We think we've caught the dog thief," whispered Maya. Up above, she saw Derek looking down at them from the projection room.

"What did you say?" asked the police chief.

"The dog thief is locked in a storeroom downstairs. But we've got to hurry! Jerry's keeping watch. Come on!" said Maya and pulled the police chief by the arm.

When Maya and the police chief came out into the lobby, they could hear banging from below.

They rushed down the stairs. Miss Bloom and Zorba were already there. They looked surprised by the commotion.

The padlock was starting to give way from all the rough treatment it had been getting from the other side of the door.

"What's happening?" asked Miss Bloom.

"There's something in there!" said Zorba.

"What's going on?" called Derek from the top step. He came limping down the stairs. He had a bulky cast covering half his leg and held the banister for support.

So that's why he's been taking a taxi to work, thought Maya.

"We think the dog thief is inside and trying to get out," replied Jerry.

"The dog thief? Who could it be?" asked

Miss Bloom. "The staff are the only ones who have access to the key to that room. Or I should say *had,* because the key has disappeared. And it would mean it's one of us . . . and there's only one person not here . . . so it must be . . . !"

Now it was the police chief's turn to be confused.

"But that lazybones is up in the auditorium, watching the movie—as if *that's* his job," he said. "I don't think I've ever seen a worse employee. I wanted to buy a bag of chocolate Kisses from him, but he refused to look at me, no matter how much I waved. And during the movie he sat right in the front the entire time, not moving a muscle."

The police chief looked at Maya and Jerry, but they didn't really understand what was going on either.

Just then the door opened with a crash. The padlock flew through the air and out

tumbled—Popcorn Pete!

"But! You're sitting up there," said the police chief and pointed toward the theater.

Popcorn Pete straightened up. All that effort had made him very red in the face. He tried to rush past, but the police chief grabbed him in an iron grip.

"Well now," said the police chief calmly, hanging on to the struggling man. "Why don't we ask "Mr. Chocolate Kisses" here to explain himself. Are you the one who steals dogs and torments their owners? And if that's the case, who on earth is up in the theater?"

"*Nobody,* of course!" scoffed Popcorn Pete.

"I put my hat on the back of the seat so that nobody would notice when I left the theater. Then I slide down to the floor and creep out through the emergency exit."

Popcorn Pete continued angrily, "It would have worked this time, too, if this blasted door hadn't gotten jammed. Now I'll never pay off my debts. I'll probably have to give the whole system back, too."

"What are you talking about?" asked the police chief.

"My home entertainment system, obviously. Eight speakers—surround sound, of course, a sixty-inch flat-screen TV—the works!"

"Your interest in movies has gone too far," said the police chief. "You'll definitely have to return that entertainment system—and the money—but let's start with the most important thing. You must return the dogs you've stolen! Their owners have been worried sick."

"Goodness gracious!" said Miss Bloom suddenly. "What's the time? The movie will be finishing soon."

"Ask Zorba," said Maya craftily.

Zorba pulled up his sleeve and then realized his mistake. There, for everyone to see, were two playing cards tucked under his watch strap.

"So that's it! That's how you do it!" exclaimed Miss Bloom. *"Fortune comes and fortune goes . . . and lucky Zorba knows no woes!* Well, thanks a lot."

Zorba looked down at the floor. He was obviously ashamed of himself.

The discovery of Zorba's cheating was interrupted by a pitiful whining.

There in the doorway of the storeroom were four small, shivering dogs. They looked back and forth between the Rio staff, the police chief, the two young detectives, and the man who had stuffed them into a sack.

The little poodle looked especially sad. He was whimpering and whining.

"Oh dear," said the police chief. "This is urgent. This little fellow must be looking for a lamppost."

Jerry crouched down and whistled to the poodle. The poodle immediately howled in reply and started toward him.

On his way across the floor, he stopped to lift his back leg and relieve himself against Popcorn Pete's pant leg.

After Doodle Bug finished his business, the police chief lead the dog thief away with a firm grip on his arm.

Miss Bloom and Zorba took the dogs upstairs and started to call their owners.

"I bet she's going to give him an earful," said Maya.

Just then the doors to the theater opened. Jerry and Maya walked out with Bert Anderson and the other moviegoers as they left the Rio Cinema.

The next day Ivy Rose and everyone else in the town of Pleasant Valley woke to read the following news:

STOLEN DOGS FOUND

The singing poodle, Doodle Bug, and his three canine companions have finally been reunited with their owners. Thanks to Maya and Jerry, Pleasant Valley's own doggy detectives, the mystery of the missing mutts was solved before the little creatures came to any harm.

The culprit? Popcorn Pete from the Rio Cinema. Instead of selling snacks, he was striking fear into the dog owners of Pleasant Valley. The reason for his crime? To pay for a top-of-the-line, very expensive home-entertainment system. "Popcorn Pete will have to change his viewing habits," joked the police chief. "The prison has a small black-and-white TV–and it even works ... sometimes!"